TEENAGE MUTANT NINJA TURTLES™

THE SECRET

story by Steve and Sónia Murphy
illustrated by Bob Ostrom

Ready-to-Read

Simon Spotlight
New York   London   Toronto   Sydney

SIMON SPOTLIGHT
An imprint of Simon & Schuster Children's Publishing Division
1230 Avenue of the Americas, New York, New York 10020
© 2004 Mirage Studios, Inc. *Teenage Mutant Ninja Turtles*™
is a trademark of Mirage Studios, Inc. All rights reserved.

Manufactured in the United States of America

First Edition

2 4 6 8 10 9 7 5 3 1

Library of Congress Cataloging-in-Publication Data
Murphy, Stephen.
The secret / by Stephen and Sónia Murphy ; illustrated by Bob Ostrom.— 1st ed.
p. cm. — (Ready-to-read)
Summary: When Raphael gives Michelangelo a cat for his birthday, Master Splinter quickly
insists that it cannot stay.
ISBN 0-689-86965-7 (pbk.)
[1. Cats—Fiction. 2. Turtles—Fiction. 3. Fear—Fiction. 4. Heroes—Fiction.] I. Murphy, Sónia.
II. Ostrom, Bob, ill. III. Teenage Mutant Ninja Turtles (Television program) IV. Title. V. Series.
PZ7.M95625 Se 2004
[Fic]—dc22
2003019179

"Surprise! Happy birthday,
   Michelangelo!" shouted Donatello,
   Raphael, Leonardo, and Splinter.
"Aww . . . and I thought you guys
   forgot!" Michelangelo said.

"Now just as soon as I blow out
these candles, we can have cake!"
Michelangelo said.
"Watch out for that spider, Mikey!"
warned Raphael.

"Ugh! Get it away from me!"
   Michelangelo yelled.
"Do not let your fears control you,
   Michelangelo," Splinter said.
"You must learn to face them."
"You are right, Master,"
   replied Michelangelo.
   Then he blew out the candles,
   and they ate the cake.

"Hey, let's open the presents!"
Raphael said.
Michelangelo opened his first gift.
It was a pair of nunchakus
from Splinter. Leonardo gave him
a photograph of martial artist
Bruce Lee.

Donatello gave Michelangelo
a Beepinator.
"It will beep every time one of your
favorite TV shows is on," he said.

"Now what could this be?"
Michelangelo asked,
opening the last gift.
"It's a cat! Thank you, Raph!"
Michelangelo said.

"I found the poor cat
wandering on the street,"
said Raphael. "He looked like
he needed some tender
loving care."
"I will call him Balloons,"
said Michelangelo.

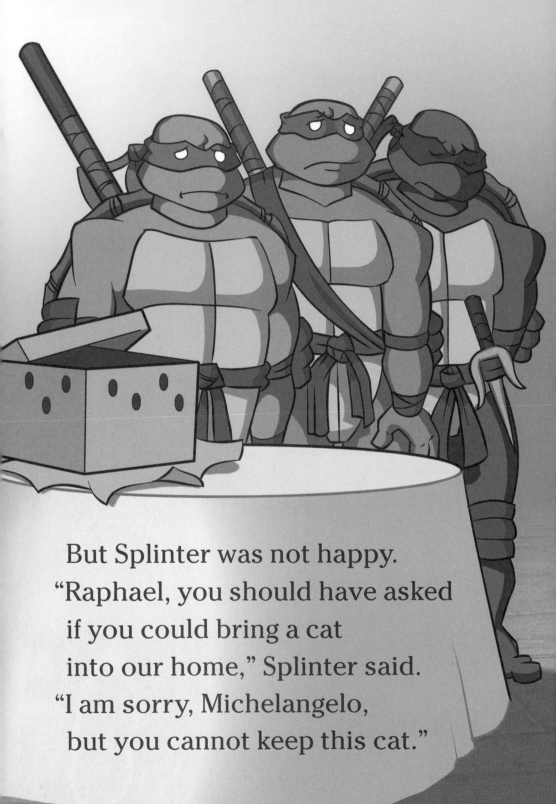

But Splinter was not happy.
"Raphael, you should have asked
if you could bring a cat
into our home," Splinter said.
"I am sorry, Michelangelo,
but you cannot keep this cat."

"But he is my birthday present!"
Michelangelo argued.
"Cats are nothing but trouble,"
replied Splinter. "The answer is no."

Raphael and Michelangelo went
to find a safe home for Balloons.
"I do not understand Master Splinter,"
Raphael said.
"Me either," Michelangelo replied.
"I do not want to give up Balloons."

"Hey, we can keep him
in this cubbyhole!" Raphael said.
"And we can visit him
whenever we want!"
"Great idea, Raph!" said Michelangelo.

Michelangelo visited Balloons every chance he had. The cat was the best birthday present ever!

After practice one day Raphael
and Michelangelo went to check
on Balloons.
"Look how hungry he is,"
Michelangelo said.
"We should have Donatello invent
an automatic feeder for him
so he will never go hungry."

Raphael and Michelangelo told
Donatello about hiding Balloons.
"So we need an automatic feeder,"
Michelangelo said.
"No problem," Donatello replied.

He hooked up an old computer
to pulleys, wires, pieces of metal,
and a very large spoon.
Then he attached a motorcycle
battery and a box of cat food.
"Here is the Chowzilla!" he declared.

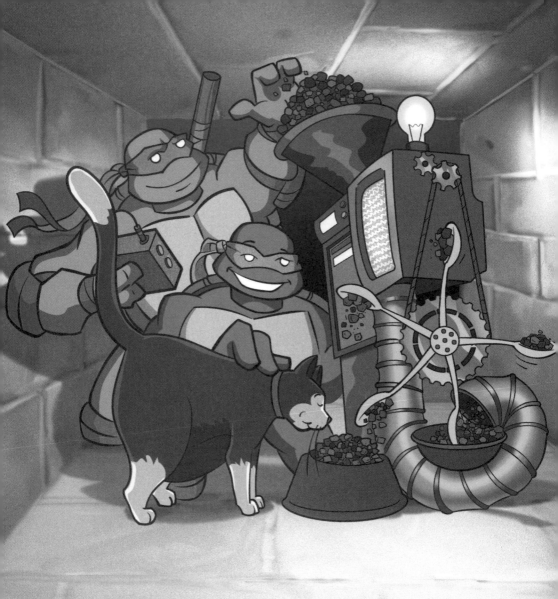

The three Turtles brought the
feeder to Balloons's hiding place.
"Here you go, little buddy,"
said Donatello, as the feeder
began to pump out cat food.

A few days later the brothers
went to visit Balloons again.
They were shocked to find cat food
all over the floor!
"Oh, no!" Donatello yelled.
"The feeder is out of control.
It's pumping cat food everywhere!"

Leonardo came over to help
clean up. "We should hurry,"
he said. "Master Splinter will be
angry that this cat is still here."
Then he added, "Say, don't you think
Balloons has gotten really fat?"

Later that day Splinter was
heading home when he found
a piece of cat food.
"Hmm, not quite the same flavor
as rat chow, but still tasty,"
he said. "Just a little fishy,
and in more ways than one."

The next day Splinter stopped
the training session to say,
"My sons, I am glad to see you
practicing. You are good students,
usually."

"'Usually'?" asked Leonardo.

"Usually," repeated Splinter.

"Come, I have something
to show you."

The Turtles followed their teacher.

Splinter led them to Balloons's hideaway. "Please explain the meaning of this," he said. "Wow!" exclaimed Michelangelo. "Balloons is a girl cat—and a mom! I just thought that we overfed her!"

"It is my fault," Michelangelo said.
"I did not want to give Balloons away.
I am sorry we kept this a secret
from you, Master."
All the Turtles felt bad.

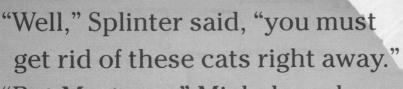

"Well," Splinter said, "you must
    get rid of these cats right away."
"But Master—," Michelangelo
    began to argue.
"No 'buts,' Michelangelo,"
    Splinter said sternly.

"But I don't understand!"
exclaimed Michelangelo.
"Why don't you like cats?"
"Not like cats?" asked Splinter.
"I did not say that I do not like cats."

Master Splinter lowered his eyes.
"My sons, I am afraid of cats,"
he said. "I remember being chased
by cats when I was a little rat."

"But you are no longer a little rat,
Master," said Michelangelo.
"Do you remember what you said
about facing one's fears?"
"You are right," Splinter agreed.
"I had ignored my own advice.
I will try to face my fears."

Over the next two days
Splinter spent his time
getting to know the cats.
"Come here, Balloons," he said.
"Come here, little kittens.
   I will no longer be afraid of you."

"What do you think, Master?"
Michelangelo asked Splinter.
"There is much a ninja can learn
from the graceful moves
of the cat," replied Splinter.

"And it's a good thing
they are not as large
as we are!" Splinter added, chuckling.
He smiled
and winked at the cats.